For Seth and Deb

Text and illustrations copyright © 1997 by Ian Wallace

Groundwood Books / Douglas & McIntyre
585 Bloor Street West
Toronto, Ontario M6G 1K5

Distributed in the U.S.A. by
Publishers Group West
4065 Hollis Street, Emeryville, CA 94608

The publisher gratefully acknowledges the assistance of the Canada Council
and the Ontario Arts Council.

Library of Congress data is available.

Canadian Cataloguing in Publication Data

Wallace, Ian, 1950-
A winter's tale

"A Groundwood book".
ISBN 0-88899-286-6

I. Title.

PS8595.A566W56 1997   jC813'.54   C97-930430-X
PZ7.W34Wi 1997

The illustrations are done in acrylics.
Design by Michael Solomon.
Printed and bound in China by Everbest Printing Co. Ltd.

A WINTER'S TALE

IAN WALLACE

❋

A GROUNDWOOD BOOK

DOUGLAS & McINTYRE

TORONTO VANCOUVER BUFFALO

THIRTEEN DAYS before Abigail's ninth birthday, her mother asked her what she wanted for a gift. Abigail didn't hesitate for even a second. She had made up her mind last January when her father and her older brother went camping together, leaving her at home for the fifth year in a row.

That cold Saturday her mother had said, "When you are nine, you'll be ready. Just like Eugene."

Abigail had waited twelve long months. She was more than ready. She had grown two inches. She had two new teeth. She could walk and even run in the snowshoes that Eugene had outgrown.

"I don't want a thing," she said. "I want to camp in the bush."

Her mother looked out the window at the bleak winter sky. An icy arctic wind blew over the city.

"I want to sleep in the snow," said Abigail.

On the Saturday of her birthday, Abigail dressed in layers of warm clothing. Then she helped her father and brother pack snowshoes and winter camping gear into the family van.

"Look at that sky, Abigail," her father said. "If the sun shone any brighter it would burst into flame like a birthday sparkler."

"And there's not one cloud to snow on your present," added Eugene.

"We'll have a great party when you get home," said her mother. She handed Abigail a camera and a bag of freshly baked cornmeal muffins.

"I wish you were coming with us, Mom," Abigail said.

"Winter camping just isn't my idea of a good time," answered her mother. She kissed Abigail on the cheek. "But I'll enjoy your photographs and the tales you'll tell."

Soon the city was ⟨...⟩
before them. And the ⟨...⟩
her father and brothe⟨...⟩
countryside.

After climbing for what seemed like hours they reached their campsite. Abigail was hungry and tired. But she ran up and across the back of an ancient rock. The beauty of the bush opened before her, a pristine landscape rolling with hills as silent as sleeping polar bears.

She took the camera from her pocket. "This one is for you, Mom," she said.

Using their snowshoes for shovels, they dug a trench in the snow, close enough to their campfire that its heat would keep them warm later that night. They lined the bottom with a thick layer of pine boughs and fashioned a lean-to of orange plastic for shelter from the wind.

Abigail leapt into the trench.

"Don't lie down," Eugene told her, "or the forest air will lull you to sleep."

"And I'll dream I'm in Heaven," she replied.

She stretched out as flat as an angel in the snow and closed her eyes. She was sure she could hear the trees whispering to each other.

A short time later they doused their campfire and headed due west to the valley where the deer ran. Abigail carried the cornmeal muffins for an afternoon snack. Along the way she took photographs to show her mother what she was missing. Her father and brother pointed out fresh tracks, deer droppings and a sheltered place where a herd had slept as recently as the night before.

"They make beds like ours!" Abigail exclaimed.

Near the base of a frozen waterfall they spotted a rack of antlers lodged in the ice. Its points stuck straight up.

Eugene smashed at the ice with his jackknife. The rack broke free. He raised it over his head. He snorted like a young buck eager to fight and charged his sister. Abigail darted in and out of the trees, her peals of laughter mixing with her brother's loud snorts.

Their noise echoed along the valley. Eugene suddenly tripped over his feet, tumbled into the deep snow, and the antlers fell out of his grasp.

By late afternoon Abigail was in the lead. Before her a frozen lake lay glinting golden in the snow. When she looked closer she saw a small shape struggling on the ice.

"Let's sneak up," her father whispered into her ear.

Cautiously, they edged their way onto the ice. Before them was a fawn twisting and pulling on something that seemed to hold it down. Suddenly sensing their presence, it stopped moving and turned to stare.

"We've got to help it, Dad," Abigail cried. "It can't get away. What's wrong?"

"I don't know yet," her father replied. "But we've got to get closer. And we must be careful. Look how terrified it is!"

They stood for a long silent moment before Abigail had an idea. She reached into the bag of muffins.

"Maybe I can get near it using these," she whispered.

She threw half a muffin like a well-shot arrow before her father or brother could answer. It landed next to the fawn. The young deer stopped struggling and leaned over. It sniffed at the food, then hungrily gobbled it up.

Closer and closer edged Abigail, throwing chunks of muffin as she went. With each bite the fawn seemed calmer and its sides stopped heaving.

Her father and brother had matched her steps. Now they could see what was trapping the young deer. Fishing line partially frozen into the ice was wound around its legs.

In one deft move Abigail's father and brother rushed forward and grabbed the fawn just as it was reaching for a chunk of muffin. The fawn struggled wildly. Her father got its head in a protective hold that would keep them both from harm.

"Quick, Abigail, quick. Grab the knife out of Eugene's pocket and cut the fishing line!" he shouted. "Do it now. Hurry!"

Abigail was afraid. The fawn was afraid. She could see the terror in its eyes and hear its panting as it twisted and turned in her father's and Eugene's arms.

She reached into Eugene's coat pocket and took out his knife. As she reached forward to cut the line, the fawn pulled away in terror. Abigail took a deep breath. Edging closer she began to cut carefully, trying not to injure its legs. Her hands had stopped shaking, and slowly but surely she cleared away the fishing line, until finally the young deer leapt free.

Abigail stared after the fawn. She felt as though she might cry, even though she had never been so happy.

As they climbed out of the valley of the deer, the sun was falling in the sky. Abigail, her father and brother turned back for one last look.

Abigail raised her camera. "Mom will like this picture."

"And the story that goes with it even more," added Eugene.

That night Abigail lay between Eugene and her father on their pine-bough bed and closed her eyes. She whispered to the bush, "This day was the best birthday gift ever." And the trees whispered their agreement in the wind.